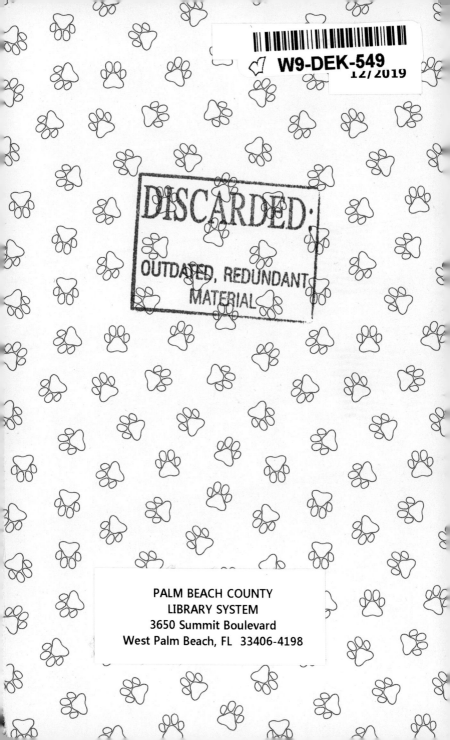

This book
belongs to

....

Muddle
The Magic Puppy

BALLET SHOW MISCHIEF

Muddle
The Magic Puppy

BALLET SHOW MISCHIEF
by Hayley Daze

Willow
Tree

This edition published by Willow Tree Books, 2018
Willow Tree Books, Tide Mill Way, Woodbridge, Suffolk, UK, IP12 1AP
First published by Ladybird Books Ltd.

0 2 4 6 8 9 7 5 3 1

Series created by Working Partners Limited,
London, WC1X 9HH
Text © 2018 Working Partners
Cover illustration © 2018 Willow Tree Books
Interior illustrations © 2018 Willow Tree Books

Special thanks to Mo O'Hara

Willow Tree Books and associated logos are trademarks and/or
registered trademarks of Tide Mill Media Ltd

ISBN: 978-1-78700-616-4
Printed and bound in Great Britain
by Bell and Bain Ltd, Glasgow

www.willowtreebooks.net

To my mom and dad
for all their love and support

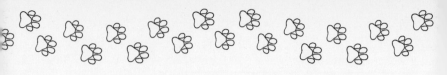

When clouds fill the sky and rain starts to fall,
Ruby and Harry are not sad at all.
They know that when puddles appear on the ground,
A magical puppy will soon be around!

Muddle's his name, he's the one
Who can lead you to worlds of adventure and fun!
He may be quite naughty, but he's clever too,
So come follow Muddle—he's waiting for you!

Contents

Chapter One
On with the Show

"Ladies and gentlemen, the show is about to begin!" Ruby shouted from behind the plush red quilt hanging across Grandpa's living room. She closed her eyes for a moment and imagined a huge theater filled with people, calling her name.

"Ruby! Ruby!"

She waved to her imaginary fans, until she realized they sounded a lot like her cousin Harry.

"Ruby! Ruby, can you hear me? What are you doing back there?"

he asked.

"It's a surprise." Ruby giggled, and peeked around the quilt. "Ready?"

"Um, sorry, Ruby, I've got to finish this maze," Harry said, pushing his glasses back in place and burying his nose in a puzzle book.

Never mind, Ruby thought as she ducked back behind the quilt, *the show must go on.* She took a big breath and tugged on her braids for luck. Her stomach felt as if it was being tickled by fairy wings. She pulled back her pretend curtain.

"Welcome to Ruby's Enchanted Ballet," she said, holding the edges of her wrinkly tutu and curtsying like she'd seen real dancers do. The wall behind Ruby was covered with drawings of rainbows, castles, mountains, and forests. Ruby had colored them all in herself, on separate sheets of paper, and taped them together.

She twirled around on her tiptoes
with her arms high above her head. But
her socks were slippery. Her legs slid
in opposite directions, causing Ruby
to accidentally do the splits. "Ta da!"
she sang, with her arms outstretched,
turning the splits into a part of her
dance routine.

"So that's what you've been working
on all morning," Harry said, closing his
puzzle book.

Ruby pushed the "play" button on
Grandpa's music player and soft violin
music filled the air.

"Now watch me do a spinning top,"
she said, holding out her tutu and
twirling to the music.

"Those are called pirouettes," Harry corrected her, "but I think you hold your arms out like this." He got up from his chair and spun around on his toes with his arms curved in front of him, using them to help him whirl around. "Woah, that really makes you dizzy," he said, sitting down again.

"And this is my graceful swan," Ruby said. She balanced on one foot and stuck out her arms like wings.

"The real name for that is an arabesque," Harry said.

"I like my name better," Ruby replied, still on one foot. "How come you know so much about ballet?"

"My parents love watching ballet at

Muddle

The Magic Puppy

the theater, and sometimes they make me go too," Harry said.

Just then the wind blew the front door open with a BANG! Ruby's pictures were whipped from the wall. They swirled around the living room and finally fluttered to the floor.

A puppy dashed onto Ruby's stage and shook himself, spraying water everywhere.

"Muddle!" shouted Ruby, twirling on her toes in delight.

Every time it rained, Muddle the naughty little puppy appeared and swept Ruby and Harry off on a magical adventure.

"Now that's what I call an entrance," Harry said with a laugh.

Muddle tugged at the curtain until it was closed.

"I guess that means my show is over," Ruby said, taking a sweeping bow.

"But our fun has only just begun!" Harry said, chasing Muddle out into the rain.

Chapter Two
The Enchanted Forest

Muddle bounded down the path in Grandpa's backyard, sniffing at one puddle and then another. He crouched down near a big pool of water.

"Is this the right puddle?" Harry asked, before jumping in with both feet. Muddy water splashed into the air

and rained down on Harry, Ruby, and Muddle.

"I guess not," Ruby said, wringing out her braids.

Muddle rolled on the ground with his mouth open and tongue lolling from side to side. Ruby thought he looked like he was laughing.

"Very funny, Muddle," Harry said, as he cleaned his glasses. His shirt and pants were dotted with muddy spots.

Ruby leaned down and whispered in Muddle's furry ear, "That was very naughty."

The puppy raced to the biggest puddle at the end of the path. He danced circles around it, so quickly that

Muddle
The Magic Puppy

Ruby was dizzy just from watching him. At last he gave a bark, leaped into the puddle and disappeared.

I wonder where we'll go this time, Ruby thought, standing at the edge of the puddle. "Are you ready?" she asked Harry. She swung her arms back and rose onto her tiptoes.

"You go first," Harry said, and gave her a playful shove.

Ruby closed her eyes—and jumped!

***

Muddle
The Magic Puppy

When Ruby opened her eyes, she had landed in what seemed to be a shadowy forest. Muddle whined nervously and snuggled close to her legs.

"Where's Harry?" Ruby asked Muddle, giving him a comforting pat on the head. "Maybe he didn't jump."

She spun in a slow circle. Harry was nowhere to be seen. "We can't go on an adventure without Harry," Ruby said.

She felt a tap on her shoulder, which made her jump. She turned around. "Harry!"she squealed. Even though Ruby loved magic, this appearing and disappearing took a little getting used to.

"This doesn't look like a very colorful adventure," Harry said, as he tucked in his shirt. "It's dark here."

"Lots of adventures start in a spooky forest," Ruby said. As her eyes adjusted,

she thought she could see twisted tree branches and thick thorns all around them. "At least, I think we're in a forest."

Muddle started to sniff. He immediately ducked behind Ruby's legs again.

"Ruby," Harry said, "did you see something move over there?"

Ruby squinted. She could just make out a tall shape moving toward them. It seemed to be hunched over, with tattered black wings. Ruby thought she could see long hair and what looked like a big crooked nose. Then the creature stopped. The dark figure raised what appeared to be a magic

Muddle
The Magic Puppy

wand, and pointed it right at Ruby.

"I can see it," Ruby whispered to Harry, "and it can definitely see us."

Chapter Three
Harry Disappears

"Eeeeeeeeeeek!" Ruby screamed, running toward Harry.

"Aaaaaaaaaaah!" Harry shouted, rushing toward Ruby.

"Wooooooooof!" Muddle barked, running around in circles.

The terrified cousins bumped right

into each other. "Quick!" Ruby said. "Which way should we go?"

"Here, through these trees," Harry said as he tried to shove the branches out of his way. The branches didn't move, but somehow the whole forest seemed to wobble. Muddle growled at the trees that were blocking his path.

"We can't get out." Ruby pushed at the trees, but instead of rough bark she felt a smooth curtain. "Do you think that creature cast a spell?" Ruby asked.

"Maybe it's some kind of force field, like in a space movie," Harry suggested, holding out his hands to inspect the strange forest.

Muddle
The Magic Puppy

Ruby glanced back. "The creature is getting closer," she whispered.

But Harry didn't answer. He'd disappeared again!

Muddle barked and clawed at the ground with his paws. Ruby dropped to her knees and tried to find the spot where Harry had vanished. Muddle growled as the dark figure approached. Her heart pounding, Ruby found what seemed to be the bottom of the forest wall. She slid her hands under and lifted it up.

"It's like a magic trapdoor," she said, as she wriggled underneath. Muddle yelped and crawled after her.

Suddenly it was daylight. Ruby

blinked as Harry came into focus. She looked behind her to see if the strange creature had followed. But now the forest had disappeared! Ruby shook her head. It was all too confusing! In place of the forest was just a plain white curtain.

"Where are we?" Ruby asked Harry, as he pulled her to her feet.

"I'm not sure, but we aren't alone," Harry said. A smiling girl was staring at Ruby.

The girl was dressed in a leotard, tights, and pink ballet shoes, complete with silky ribbons tied around her ankles. Her blond hair was brushed back into a bun on the top of her head,

except for one curl that hung down
by the side of her face. She twisted it
around her finger as she spoke. "Where
did you come from?"

"We could ask you the same thing," Ruby said. She tried to smile, but her body was still buzzing from the fright of the shadowy forest and the scary creature.

"Something followed us here," Harry added. "I think we need to hide."

"See, Muddle agrees," Ruby said, as the puppy tugged at the silky ribbons on the girl's shoes, trying to pull her along but accidentally untying them.

"What on earth are you doing here?" said a cross voice from behind them.

"I think it's too late for hiding," the girl said with a gulp.

Muddle
The Magic Puppy

Chapter Four
The Magic of the Stage

A tall lady in a dark leotard and long skirt walked over. She frowned at Ruby, Harry, and Muddle. "You've interrupted the final dress rehearsal for my ballet."

"Dress rehearsal?" Ruby said.

"Of course," Harry said, looking around. "We're in a theater! This is the

stage," he said, pointing at the wooden floorboards under their feet.

"But where's the forest?" Ruby asked, scratching her head.

"It's painted on the backdrop that you just crawled under," said the lady. "Look." She clapped her hands and gestured to someone at the side of the stage.

The plain backdrop next to them flew into the air. Muddle barked at the vanishing curtain. As they stood underneath it, they could see the twisted trees of the forest painted on the back of the curtain. There was another forest painted on a curtain at the back of the stage too.

The lady clapped again, and the huge red velvet curtain at the front of the stage opened. Ruby, Harry, and Muddle stared out in amazement at the rows and rows of seats in front of them.

"I am Miss Sue," the lady continued. "And this is Elizabeth." The girl in the leotard curtsied. "Would you kindly tell me who you are and what you are doing here?"

"I'm Ruby," Ruby replied, "This is my

cousin Harry, and this is Muddle. We were trying to escape from a terrifying creature."

"You mean that creature?" Elizabeth said, giggling as she pointed behind them.

Ruby and Harry turned to see a slightly taller girl standing in the bright spotlights. She was wearing a green wig, a bumpy pretend nose, and wings made of lace.

"I'm Kate," the girl said. "I'm only pretending to be a scary fairy. It's my part in the ballet."

Muddle galloped over and hopped into Kate's arms. He licked her face.

"I was never really scared," Harry said, but he looked relieved.

"The girls were just about to rehearse their dance for *Sleeping Beauty*," Miss Sue said. "You can watch from the wings, if you like."

"The wings..." Ruby repeated, searching for feathers.

"That's what they call the sides of the stage that the audience can't see," Elizabeth said, taking her position with Kate on the stage.

Miss Sue signalled for the music to start as Ruby, Harry, and Muddle rushed offstage. They watched the girls

twirl and whirl together. They sprang
so high into the air it was as if their
feet were made of springs. Muddle's tail
wagged in time to the music.

"Elizabeth looks just like a gazelle

when she jumps. I wish I could dance like that," Ruby whispered to Harry. "Gazelle, gazelle, froggy jump, gazelle, gazelle, spinning top," she said quietly to herself.

"What are you doing?" Harry asked, leaning in close to Ruby.

"I'm memorizing Elizabeth's dance so I can do it when we get back home," Ruby replied. "Froggy jump, gazelle, spinning top, spinning top."

Muddle barked and hopped across the stage on his back legs.

"Look, Muddle's dancing too," Elizabeth said, laughing as the dance came to an end.

"Maybe Muddle will make his debut tonight as well," said Kate, nudging Elizabeth.

"Could I help make a 'debut?' I'm very good at making things," Ruby said.

"You make a 'debut' when you

perform your first lead role in a show," explained Kate.

Miss Sue nodded. "And Elizabeth is making her debut today as the princess."

"Yes," said Elizabeth. "Later in the show I have to dance on the stage all by myself." There was a slight tremble in her voice and she twisted her curl of hair around and around her finger.

"I'm sure you'll be great, Elizabeth," Harry said, pushing his glasses back into place.

Miss Sue checked her watch. "My stars, look at the time. Please clear the stage, everyone. The audience will be here soon."

As Elizabeth looked out at the empty theater, Ruby thought she spotted a tear in her eye.

What could be wrong with the star of the show?

Muddle
The Magic Puppy

Chapter Five
Hidden Treasures

As Elizabeth walked offstage with Ruby, Harry, and Muddle, she whispered, "I've never performed in front of a proper audience before. What if I make a mistake?"

"Lots of performers get stage fright," Harry interrupted. "Try not to worry

about it."

"I know you're right," Elizabeth said, wrapping her stray curl around her finger again. "But I can't help it."

"Excuse me!" They all stepped aside as a man dressed in black, carrying a giant painted nutcracker, hurried past. "Better get this out of the way." He headed toward the stairs at the back of the stage. Muddle raced after him.

"Wait, Muddle," Ruby called after the naughty puppy.

"Muddle's got the right idea," Elizabeth said, brightening. "Do you want to see the most amazing thing ever?"

Elizabeth, Ruby, Harry, and Muddle followed the man down a winding staircase. They stayed close behind him as he snaked around the theater's basement. Harry had to drag Ruby along because she wanted to stop and look at everything. They passed a clothes rack full of pirate costumes with polished brass buttons. Around the corner was a fluffy white object on a stand.

"What's that?" asked Ruby, pointing. "It looks like a powdered poodle."

Muddle hunched down and growled at the white furry thing.

Elizabeth giggled. "It's not a poodle—it's a wig."

Down another corridor Ruby saw a basket full of pink ballet shoes of all different sizes. She wondered if any of the shoes would fit her. She had always wanted a pair of proper ballet shoes.

Finally, the man went into a room

with the word "Props" painted on the door.

"What does 'Props' mean?" Ruby whispered.

"Property of the theater," Harry said. "It's all the items that performers use onstage—like fake swords or magic wands."

After a moment, the man left the props room and walked away.

"Come on," said Elizabeth as she opened the door. Ruby thought the room smelled just like the arts and crafts lockers at school.

"Look at all these things," Ruby said, wide-eyed.

Muddle barked as he bounded up to

a large feather headdress and sniffed.
He sneezed and rubbed his nose with
his paws.

The room was crammed with swans'
wings, fairy wands, Spanish fans, and
jeweled crowns. Muddle rushed around
inspecting everything. There was an

oversized wooden dollhouse in one corner and a large stuffed crocodile in the other. Harry noticed some rose bushes leaning against the wall.

"They look so real," he said, touching them. "Ouch! Right down to the thorns."

Ruby gazed up at a giant lollipop with yellow and red swirls. "I wish this was real," she said "I bet it would taste like banana and strawberry."

"That's from *The Nutcracker*—one of my favorite ballets," Elizabeth said. "But this is my favorite thing in the entire props room." She pulled back a huge white sheet to reveal a pumpkin carriage on golden wheels.

"It's Cinderella's magic coach!" Ruby said, jumping up and down with excitement. "Can we go inside?"

"Of course," Elizabeth said.

Ruby and Elizabeth climbed into the carriage while Harry sat with Muddle at the front, pretending to hold the

reins of imaginary horses. Ruby waved
out of the window and imagined she
was Cinderella on her way to the ball.

Ruby was jolted from her
daydream by a voice booming over the

loudspeaker: "Miss Elizabeth to the dressing room, please."

"I've got to get ready," said Elizabeth, hurrying out of the pumpkin carriage.

Ruby and Harry draped the sheet back over the carriage, careful to leave everything just as they found it. They all raced out of the props room and down the corridor—until they came to another corridor that looked exactly the same.

"I can't remember which way we came," Harry said, scratching his head. "We just followed that man carrying the nutcracker. I wasn't paying that much attention."

Muddle paced up and down.

"It's a maze down here. We'll never get back in time for the show," Elizabeth said. "We're lost!"

Chapter Six
A Crazy Maze

"That's it," said Harry.

"That's it? You're giving up?" Ruby exclaimed.

"No—that's it! Elizabeth just said that it's a maze down here, and I'm good at mazes. I do them in my puzzle books all the time." Harry adjusted his

glasses. "We can work this out. We just have to remember what we saw on the way in, and look for those things on the way out."

"Pirate clothes, poodle wigs...oh, what was next?" Ruby said.

Harry read a sign on the wall. It had arrows pointing in every direction. "Well, this way is a workshop, and down there is the shoe room," Harry said.

"I remember!" Ruby shouted. "Pirate clothes, poodle wigs, and pretty princess pumps!"

Ruby, Harry, Elizabeth, and Muddle walked quickly down the corridor. But they couldn't find the pirate clothes

from Ruby's list.

"This isn't the right way," Elizabeth said, twisting the stray curl around her finger.

"Wait a minute," said Harry. "We have to do the list in reverse. It's not, 'pirate clothes, poodle wigs, and pretty princess pumps'—it's 'princess pumps, poodle wigs, and pirate clothes'."

"Harry, you're a genius!" Elizabeth exclaimed.

"And there are the ballet shoes!" Ruby cried, running down the corridor, past the overflowing baskets of pink

ballet slippers.

"And there's the powdered wig that looks like a big white poodle," Elizabeth said as they turned the corner. They continued until they reached another turning point.

"There are the pirate clothes," Elizabeth said, clapping her hands. "We did it!"

Right at the end of the corridor was Miss Sue, standing by the dressing room door and tapping her watch. "My stars, Elizabeth. What's kept you?"

"Sorry," Elizabeth said as they filed into the dressing room. Elizabeth stood, not moving, in front of the dressing

room mirror while the other dancers got ready.

"You've got to get ready," Ruby said.

She spotted the pole with tutus stacked on top of each other. "Which one is yours?" she asked Elizabeth.

Elizabeth pointed to a pretty blue tutu decorated with yellow flowers. Ruby held the tutu steady while Elizabeth stepped into it. Elizabeth twisted her lock of hair around her finger, faster and faster.

"There's no need to be nervous now," Harry said. "We made it in time."

Ruby noticed that all the other girls wore their hair in neat buns that shimmered with glitter. She smoothed back Elizabeth's hair and clipped her over-twirled strand into place.

"Now for the finishing touch," Ruby

said. She picked up the pot of glitter.
Muddle scampered over to inspect
it. The puppy took a big sniff and
then sneezed a glittery burst all over
Elizabeth, Ruby, and Harry.

"Oops! We'll just have to be extra
sparkly," Ruby said. Muddle sneezed
another splash of sparkles.

Muddle
The Magic Puppy

"It's time, Elizabeth," said Miss Sue. "Ready?"

Elizabeth tagged along behind Miss Sue and the other dancers.

"Break a leg!" Harry called out after Elizabeth.

"Harry!" gasped Ruby. "What a horrible thing to say."

"People in the theater say it to each other all the time. It means good luck," Harry explained.

Ruby giggled and tugged her braids to give Elizabeth some extra luck.

Ruby, Harry, and Muddle waited until the dressing room was empty, then they made their way to the wings to watch. The red velvet front curtain

was shut, but Kate was already on the stage. Muddle raced onto the stage and circled Kate.

"Woof! Woof!" Muddle barked up at Ruby and Harry.

"Wait—Muddle's right. Something's wrong," Ruby said.

"Where's Elizabeth?" Harry asked. "This is the part of the ballet where she dances with Kate, isn't it?"

Miss Sue paced back and forth, looking for Elizabeth. She shook her head sadly, and Kate lifted her arms to start the dance.

"Oh no," said Ruby. "Without Elizabeth, the ballet will be ruined!"

Chapter Seven
Spinning in the Spotlight

"Maybe the ballet won't be ruined after all," said Harry, nudging Ruby toward the stage.

Muddle barked and pulled at Ruby's tutu. Miss Sue walked up to Ruby. "The show must go on," she said, handing Ruby a pair of ballet shoes.

"But I can't dance in front of all those people," Ruby said, peeking through the curtain at the audience.

"You love to dance," Harry said. "Now's your chance."

Ruby took a deep breath, kicked off her boots, slipped on the ballet shoes, and twirled onto the stage.

The red curtain opened and the audience clapped. Ruby remembered her names for Elizabeth's dance steps. "Gazelle, gazelle, froggy jump," she repeated to herself. "Gazelle, gazelle, spinning top."

Ruby couldn't believe it. She was dancing in a real ballet! Kate smiled at her as they both glided around the

stage.

When Ruby performed her final
swan move and gracefully slid into the
splits, the crowd clapped and cheered.

Ruby tried to take a picture of this moment in her mind. She wanted to remember all the smiling faces.

Ruby walked back into the wings and Miss Sue gave her a big smile, as if to say thank you. But before Ruby could smile back, ballerinas in white tutus rushed past her onto the stage, taking their positions for the next dance.

Muddle hopped on his back legs until Ruby leaned down so he could give her a big lick on the nose.

"You were great," Harry said. "But we have to find Elizabeth before her big solo!"

Ruby nodded. "Let's think...where could she be?"

Muddle barked and headed for the stairs. "I bet he's right," Harry said. "Come on!" They ran after the puppy.

"Now, which way was it?" Harry asked.

"Pirate clothes, poodle wigs, and

pretty princess pumps!" they both sang out together, and ran all the way to the props room. Inside, Muddle trotted over to Cinderella's pumpkin carriage and pointed a paw. Ruby noticed that the white sheet had been taken off the carriage. "I think Elizabeth's inside," she said to Harry.

Ruby knocked gently on the carriage door. "Elizabeth? Are you in there?"

The door slowly opened and Elizabeth stepped out. Muddle rubbed against her legs. She leaned down to stroke his ear.

"I'm sorry. I can't do my solo," she said. "There are so many people in the audience. I'm scared."

"But Kate and all your friends are counting on you. You have to try," said Harry.

Elizabeth simply shook her head and started twisting her hair around her

finger again.

"You were fine dancing when Harry and I were watching, weren't you?" said Ruby.

Elizabeth nodded.

"Then what if Harry and I are onstage and you just dance for us?" Ruby suggested.

"But how can we be onstage without being seen by the audience?" Harry asked. He leaned on the fake rose bushes next to him. "Ouch! These thorns hurt!"

"We can put the rose bushes at the front of the stage and hide behind them," Ruby said. "Now you see me..." she ducked behind one of the bushes,

"now you don't!"

"I guess I can try," Elizabeth said.

"Then let's go," Ruby said.

Harry and Ruby each grabbed one of the pretend rose bushes, and they hurried back up to the stage.

"You can do it," Ruby said, hugging Elizabeth.

Harry gave Elizabeth a big thumbs up. Muddle nudged her toward the other dancers. Elizabeth nodded and flitted to the center of the stage.

Ruby, Harry, and Muddle hid behind the rose bushes and slowly crept to the front of the stage amid a flurry of tutus. The other dancers circled around Elizabeth, then danced off the sides of

the stage. The curtain opened. This was her big moment! But instead of beginning her dance, Elizabeth stood frozen to the spot, staring out at the audience.

"Oh, no," Ruby whispered to Harry. "She's too scared to dance!"

Muddle

The Magic Puppy

Chapter Eight
The Curtain Call

"We need to get Elizabeth to look at us, not the audience," Harry said.

Muddle hopped up on his back legs, just as he had done in the rehearsal. Only this time, he was hidden by the bushes. Ruby waved to Elizabeth and then pointed at Muddle, who was

hopping in time to the music. The sight made Elizabeth smile, and she began to dance.

When she finished, cries of "Bravo!" echoed around the theater. As the dancers took their bows, the audience tossed flowers onto the stage.

"It's raining roses," Ruby said. Muddle grabbed a single red rose in his mouth. He headed straight for Elizabeth and placed the rose at her feet.

"Thanks, Muddle." Elizabeth was grinning from ear to ear. She patted Muddle on the head and took another

bow with the other dancers.

Miss Sue walked onto the stage and
motioned for Harry and Ruby to join
her. The cousins came out of hiding and
faced the audience. Harry bowed. As
Ruby curtsied, she slipped on the stage
and ended up doing the splits. The
crowd cheered.

"I couldn't have done it without
your help," Elizabeth whispered to Ruby
and Harry. "You two saved the show.
Oh, and Muddle, of course!"

Just then, Muddle trotted over to
the front curtain and started to pull it
closed.

"I think Muddle's trying to tell us
that it's time to go," Ruby said, as the

velvety curtain swung shut.

Ruby and Harry dashed offstage. Ruby slipped off her ballet shoes. She wished she could take them with her, but she pulled on her boots instead.

Muddle began to race around Harry and Ruby. The world went fuzzy. Ruby felt as if someone was tickling her all over.

"Goodbye," called Miss Sue, Kate, and Elizabeth. "Thanks for everything!"

***

When Ruby opened her eyes, she and Harry were once again in Grandpa's backyard. She splashed in every puddle on the path to the house. She fluttered her arms like a butterfly. Spun like a top. Kicked like a kangaroo. And then

swayed her arms in the air like a tree in the wind.

"What are you doing?" Harry asked, staring at Ruby over the top of his rain-splattered glasses.

"I'm making up a new dance for when I'm a world famous ballerina," Ruby said with a bow.

"Just make sure you wipe your muddy feet before you go inside Grandpa's house," Harry said, and demonstrated wiping his feet on the wet grass. "I call this move 'the charging bull'." He lowered his head and bolted toward the front door.

"I call that 'my crazy cousin'," Ruby muttered.

Harry stumbled over the welcome mat. "Hey, what's this?"

Ruby picked up a pair of pink slippers with long, silky ribbons.

"Proper ballet shoes!" she squealed. She recognized the muddy paw prints on the mat. "Thanks, Muddle!" she called into the rainy breeze. She tugged her braids for luck and wished for more rain.

Muddle
The Magic Puppy

Can't wait to find out
what Muddle will do next?
Then read on! Here is the first
chapter from Muddle's fourth
adventure, Rainforest Hide
and Go Seek...

Muddle
The Magic Puppy

RAINFOREST HIDE AND GO SEEK

"I'm a water fairy!" Ruby cried, wrapping a damp strand of feathery pondweed around her head and sticking a pink water lily behind one ear. "And I can make myself invisible."

Her braids bounced as she waved her fishing net like a magic wand.

Ruby's cousin Harry stared at her.

"I can still see you," he said, pushing his glasses up his nose. He lifted his fishing net out of Grandpa's pond and peered into it. "I've caught something!" he exclaimed.

"Let me look." Ruby raced over to Harry and peered inside the bulging, dripping net. "It's just lots of pondweed and tiny bits of sticks and stone," she said.

But then the pondweed moved. A little green frog sitting among the leaves began to ribbit.

"Wow!" Ruby said. "He's the exact

same color as the pondweed."

"It's called camouflage," Harry said. He flicked through his favorite wildlife book which was lying open at the pond-life page. "Lots of creatures use it to blend in with their surroundings, so no one can see them."

"Like they're invisible," Ruby said, smiling.

Ruby and Harry carefully tipped the frog onto a lily pad.

Ruby's pondweed crown fell off as she lay on her belly at the edge of the pond and watched the frog hop from leaf to leaf.

Two electric-blue dragonflies whizzed and hovered overhead. Then

a series of ripples spread out across the water.

Plop, plop...plop, plop...plop.

Ruby's heart leaped for joy. Huge raindrops were plopping into the pond, bouncing off the lily pads. Water dripped from her braids as she sat up. "Where's Muddle?" she asked.

Whenever it rained, their magic puppy friend arrived, and they went on amazing adventures.

On the far side of the pond, a clump of rushes rustled.

"Woof! Woof!" Muddle bounded out of the rushes toward Ruby and Harry, wagging his tail.

"Hello, boy," Ruby said, patting

Muddle all over. "Where are you taking us today?" said Harry and Ruby together, as Muddle barked happily.

The little puppy trotted up the path in Grandpa's backyard, where the rain had already made large puddles.

Ruby held her breath. She wondered which puddle the puppy would choose. When Muddle was around, a rainy puddle could become the gateway to a new and exciting magical adventure.

Muddle stopped at the largest pool of water, ran around it, jumped in—and

disappeared.

Ruby turned to Harry and shouted, "One, two, three, JUMP!"

And into the puddle they went.

***

To be continued...